JULIA DONALDSON

The Quick Brown Fox Cub

Illustrated by LUCY RICHARDS

Crabtree Publishing Company
www.crabtreebooks.com

PMB 16A, 350 Fifth Avenue,   616 Welland Avenue,
Suite 3308,   St. Catharines, Ontario
New York, NY 10118   Canada, L2M 5V6

For Isla
J.D.

For Grandad Pop
L.R.

Donaldson, Julia.
  The quick brown fox cub / written by Julia Donaldson ; illustrated by Lucy Richards.
    p. cm. -- (Red bananas)
  Summary: When his mother moves their family to the city, Frisk, an adventurous fox
cub, gets excited about exploring and, instead of sleeping during the day when it is safe,
he begins following a girl to school and learning about "magic white marks" called letters.
  ISBN-13: 978-0-7787-1080-6 (rlb) -- ISBN-10: 0-7787-1080-7 (rlb)
  ISBN-13: 978-0-7787-1096-7 (pbk) -- ISBN-10: 0-7787-1096-3 (pbk)
  1. Foxes--Juvenile fiction. [1. Foxes--Fiction. 2. Adventure and adventurers--Fiction. 3.
Human-animal relationships--Fiction. 4. Television--Fiction. 5. Books and reading-
Fiction.] I. Richards, Lucy, ill. II. Title. III. Series.
  PZ10.3.D71495Qui 2006
  [E]--dc22   2005035775 LC

Published by Crabtree Publishing in 2006
First published in 2005 by Egmont Books Ltd.
Text copyright © Julia Donaldson 2005
Illustrations copyright © Lucy Richards 2005
The Author and Illustrator have asserted their moral rights.
Paperback ISBN 0-7787-1096-3
Reinforced Hardcover Binding ISBN 0-7787-1080-7

Contents

Red Bananas

A New Home

Frisk was a quick brown fox cub. He lived with his mother, his brother, and his sister in a home called

The Old Burrow
The Tree Roots
The Edge of the Wood
The Country.

Frisk was a big worry to his mother. He was always running off by himself to look for rabbits.

How many times do I have to tell you?

Sorry, Mom.

"Why can't you stay and play with the others?" Mom scolded him. "Do you want the fox hunters to catch you like they caught your dad?"

"Sorry, Mom," Frisk said, but a minute later he was off again.

In the end, his Mom was so worried that one evening she told the cubs, "We're moving to town."

"What's town?" Frisk asked.

"It's a nice place with no hunters," said Mom. "I used to live there before I met your dad."

Let's go!

"Does town have rabbits?" asked Frisk.

"We won't need rabbits. There's lots of other food in town," said Mom.

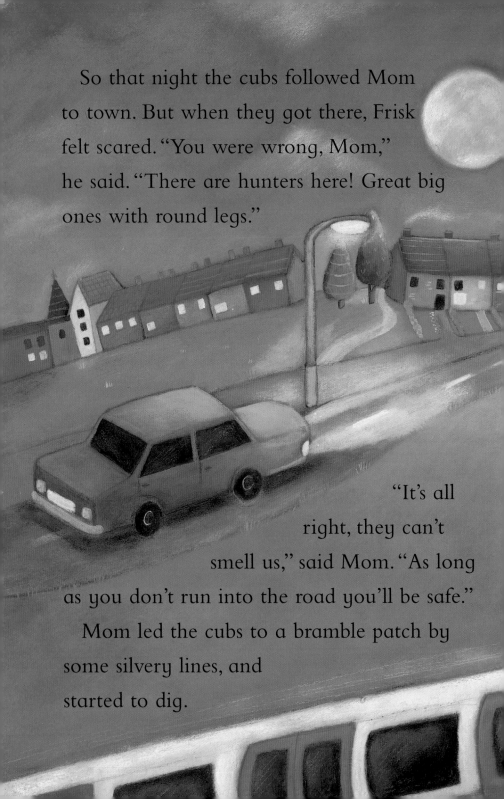

So that night the cubs followed Mom to town. But when they got there, Frisk felt scared. "You were wrong, Mom," he said. "There are hunters here! Great big ones with round legs."

"It's all right, they can't smell us," said Mom. "As long as you don't run into the road you'll be safe."

Mom led the cubs to a bramble patch by some silvery lines, and started to dig.

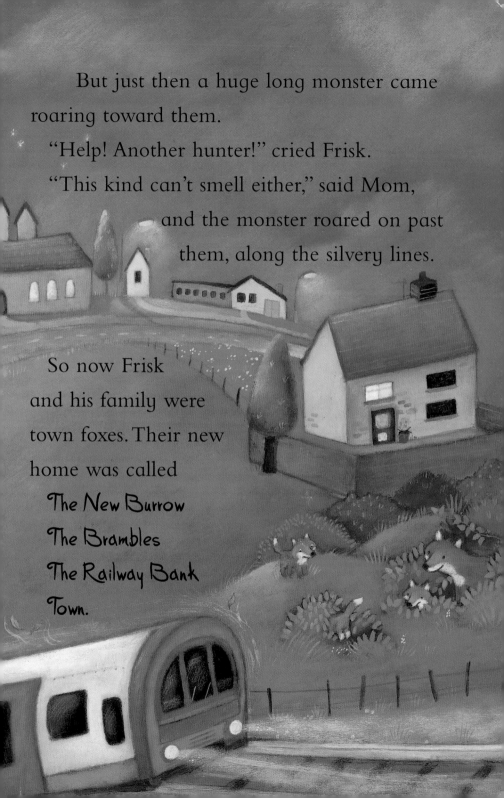

But just then a huge long monster came roaring toward them.

"Help! Another hunter!" cried Frisk.

"This kind can't smell either," said Mom, and the monster roared on past them, along the silvery lines.

So now Frisk and his family were town foxes. Their new home was called
The New Burrow
The Brambles
The Railway Bank
Town.

Magic Rabbits

"It's dinner time," said Mom.
She jumped over a wall and the
cubs followed her. They landed
in a garden with a wooden
table in the middle of it.

"What's that?" asked Frisk.

"It's a fox table,"
said Mom.
On top of the table
the foxes found
some bread and
bacon rinds.
They ate them all up.

Fox food!

"What's for dessert?" asked Frisk.

"Follow me," said Mom, and she took them to a big black bin.

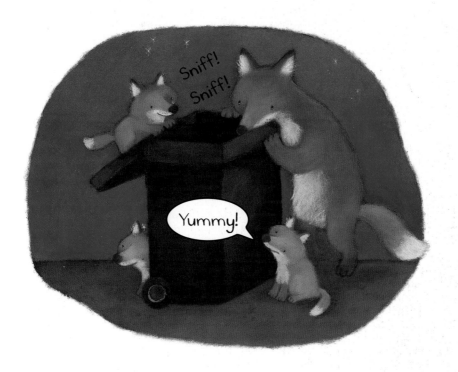

"It's a fox bin," she told them. She nosed the lid off it and they found some more fox food inside, as well as some nice cans for the cubs to play with. They ate and played until the sky began to grow light.

"It's bedtime," said Mom.
"I don't want to go to bed.
I want to do some more
exploring," said Frisk,
but Mom told him he
would have to wait.
"Nights are for exploring.
Days are for sleeping,"
she said, and she led
the cubs back to their new
home in the bramble patch.

Frisk woke up before the others. It was still light, but he couldn't wait to go exploring again. He left Mom and the others sleeping, and jumped over the wall into the garden.

Near the fox bin he saw a door with a flap in the bottom of it.

"It must be a fox flap!" said Frisk. He nosed it open and bounded through it into a room. There was a bowl of fox food on the floor. Frisk ate it all up. It tasted even better than the food on the fox table or in the fox bin.

Just then he heard a voice. "Thanks for joining us on Fur and Feathers," it said. "Today we're looking at rabbits."

13

Rabbits! That sounded good. Frisk crept toward the voice, into another room. A girl was sitting on a chair with a cat on her lap.

The cat was asleep, but the girl was watching a big square shiny box.

Frisk looked at the box too. It was full of rabbits! He let out a yelp of excitement.

Then three things happened at once.

The cat
jumped down,

the girl
turned around,

and the rabbits in the
box turned into a man!

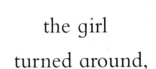

Frisk ran. He bounded through the fox flap and all the way back to his new home. He pounced on his sister to wake her up.

Hey, listen!

Go back to sleep.

"Mom was wrong. There are rabbits in town," he told her. "Magic ones that can turn into people!"

"Don't be silly – it was just a dream," said his sister.

16

Magic Marks

That night the foxes ate and played in the garden again. Just as they were about to go home to bed, they heard one of the round-legged hunters stop outside the house.

"Help! Maybe they can smell us after all!" said Frisk. But Mom didn't look scared. "That sounds like a fox van to me," she said, and she led the cubs around to the front of the house. The fox van had driven off, but on the front doorstep stood three cartons.

"What's inside them?" asked Frisk.

"Fox milk," said Mom. She bit a hole in one of the cartons and tipped it over. The milk ran out and the foxes lapped it up.

Frisk noticed that there
was a flap in the front door
too – but it was too small
and too high up to go through.

"That's a silly fox flap," he said.

Just then the door opened and out came
the girl who had been watching the magic
box. She had a bag on her back.

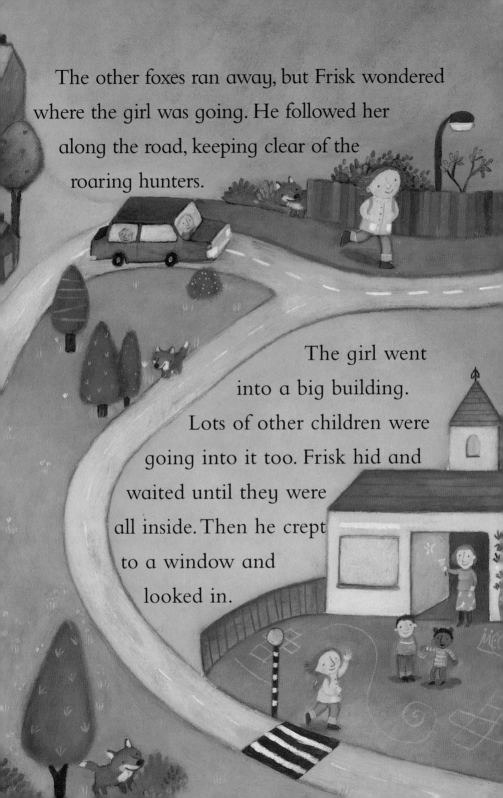

The other foxes ran away, but Frisk wondered where the girl was going. He followed her along the road, keeping clear of the roaring hunters.

The girl went into a big building. Lots of other children were going into it too. Frisk hid and waited until they were all inside. Then he crept to a window and looked in.

He saw some children sitting down and a woman standing up. The woman drew something on a black board with a small white stick. Frisk felt excited – it was a picture of a fox jumping over a dog! Then the woman made some strange marks on the board. They looked like this:

"That sentence has every letter of the alphabet in it," said the woman.

"What is she talking about?" Frisk wondered.

"Now, Jenny," said the woman. "Point to the word 'fox'."

A girl stood up. It was the one Frisk had followed! She went to the board and pointed to some of the marks.

"F – O – X. Fox," said Jenny.

"Those marks mean me!" thought Frisk, and he ran home to tell his family.

The other cubs were asleep, but Mom lay
with one eye open.

"What time of day do you call this?" she
asked Frisk.

"Sorry, Mom," said Frisk. "But I've been
exploring. And I've seen some magic marks."

Mom wasn't interested in the marks. "I keep
telling you," she scolded him, "nights are for
exploring. Days are for sleeping."

Magic Ducks

Although Frisk was the last to bed, once again he was the first one up. He felt hungry. Remembering the fox food inside the house, he bounded over the wall, across the garden, and through the fox flap.

There on the floor was the bowl of fox food, but the cat was eating it! When she saw Frisk she hissed at him.

Hiss!

Just then he heard a voice. "Thanks for joining us on Fur and Feathers," it said. "Today, we're looking at ducks."

Ducks! That sounded almost as good as rabbits. Frisk crept into the room with the magic box.

Jenny was watching it, and a dog was curled up at her feet. Frisk was scared of dogs, but this one was asleep.

This time, the magic box was full of ducks.

"I must keep quiet," thought Frisk, but when one of the ducks quacked he couldn't help running toward it. Again, three things happened at once.

The dog
woke up,

the girl
turned around,

and the ducks
turned into a woman!

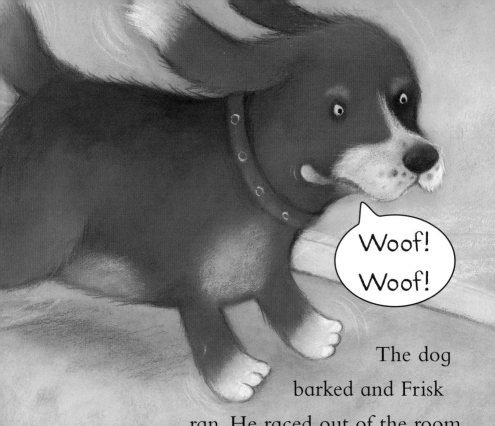

Woof!
Woof!

The dog
barked and Frisk
ran. He raced out of the room,
into the other room and toward the fox
flap. The dog was coming after him. Frisk
could hear him panting.

Frisk bounded through the fox flap. He
hoped that the dog would be too big to get
through. He felt his heart beating as he ran
across the garden and back over the wall to
the bramble patch.

Mom and the others were
still asleep. He bit his brother's
ear to wake him up. "I've been hunted," he
told him. "And I've seen some magic ducks."

"Don't be silly – it was just a dream," said
his brother.

Zzzzzz . . .

That night, Frisk felt tired. While the others were still eating and playing in the garden he slunk back to bed. He woke up when they returned in the morning.

"You've missed the fox milk," his brother told him.

"You are silly, confusing up night with day," said his sister.

Then the two of them snuggled up to Mom and went to sleep.

By now Frisk was wide awake. He decided to go and see if there was any fox milk still left on the doorstep.

There wasn't, but he was just in time to see Jenny come out of the house with her bag on her back.

Frisk started to think about
the magic white marks.

"I must see them again, I must!" he
thought, and he followed Jenny
to the big building.

Over here!

Me! Me!

Jenny went inside
with all the other children,
but this time a lot of them
came back out again and
started to run around. They
seemed to be hunting a ball. A man was
holding a silver thing that he kept blowing.

"It must be a hunting horn,"
thought Frisk.

30

Frisk went around to the back of the building and found a whole row of fox bins, full of good things. He poked his nose into a big can and licked the food from the bottom of it. Then he tried to get his nose out.

Help!

"Help! I'm stuck!" he said.
He couldn't see. He ran around and around. Now he could hear voices and feet all around him. The hunters! He didn't know which way to run.

Then a voice said, "Keep still, it's all right,"
and Frisk felt the can being pulled off his nose.

He could see now. Jenny was holding the
can, and all the children were smiling. But
the hunter was looking at him through a big
black thing. Help! Perhaps it was a gun.

Frisk ran home. His brother and sister were fast asleep, but Mom had been waiting up for him.

"How many times do I have to tell you?" she began. "Days are for . . ."

"Sleeping. I know, and I'm sorry," said Frisk. "But I did so want to see the magic marks again." Then he told Mom all about his adventure.

You and your adventures!

Mom was still angry, but she said, "I don't think the black thing was a gun."

"What was it then?" asked Frisk.

"A fox-watcher," said Mom.

The Lazy Dog

In the end, Mom gave up trying to stop Frisk confusing night with day. He just couldn't stay away from the big building. He went there every day and looked through the window. He watched the woman making the magic marks on the board and the children telling her what they meant. He learned that the marks were called letters, and he learned to read them.

34

"I can read 'The quick brown fox jumps over the lazy dog'," he told Mom proudly one night. "That's got all the letters of the alphabet in it."

Sometimes the big and small people saw him, but Frisk didn't mind, as long as they didn't come too near. He didn't even mind when they looked at him through the strange black fox-watcher.

Frisk longed to watch the magic box again. When he looked through Jenny's window he could only see the back of it. But he was too scared to go through the fox flap again, in case he met the dog.

Ruff! Ruff!

Now and then the foxes saw the dog in the garden. Sometimes he was hunting a ball or a stick that Jenny threw for him, but more often he was asleep. He was a lazy dog. Even so, Mom said it was best to keep away from him.

Frisk also kept away from the two big people who shared Jenny's house with her. He didn't like them as much as Jenny. He couldn't understand why they let birds sit on the fox table, or why they let the cat come and go through the fox flap. Even worse, they stole the fox milk for themselves unless the foxes got there first.

That's my milk!

One morning, when the foxes were waiting by the front door for the fox milk to arrive, Frisk noticed a paper thing sticking out of the silly high-up fox flap. He pulled it out.

"What's this?" he asked, but for once Mom didn't know.

"Look! There's a picture of the magic box on the front!" said Frisk. He looked inside and saw a lot of pictures and writing.

"I can read this!" he said proudly. But most of it was boring stuff about people.

Then Frisk saw some words which made his bushy tail swish.

It sounded very exciting, but what did it mean?

Just then, Jenny came out of the house and Frisk followed her to the big building. He looked through the window and saw the woman writing on the board:

Today 5 o'clock Fox Watch.

It's tonight!

"Don't forget to watch the box!" she said to the children.

Suddenly, Frisk understood. There were going to be foxes in the magic box!

"I must see them, I must!" he cried.

The Quick Brown Fox Cub

Frisk was so excited that he hardly slept a wink all day. When the others were still asleep he bounded over the wall, ran to Jenny's back door, and poked his nose through the fox flap. But there he stopped. He didn't dare go any further. He was scared of meeting the dog and being hunted again.

Just then, Jenny came into the
room and saw him peeping through
the fox flap. She put a finger on
her lips and beckoned to him.

Frisk decided to be brave.
He jumped through the fox flap.

Ssshh!

"Come on, Jenny, it's starting!" he heard
one of the big people call, and then
he heard another voice saying,
"Tonight we're looking at foxes."

Frisk crept after Jenny into the room with the magic box. The two big people were already watching it. Jenny sat down with them. The cat jumped on to her lap. Frisk looked around and felt glad that he couldn't see the dog.

Where are the foxes?

He sat behind a chair and watched the magic box. But he couldn't see any foxes. There was a man talking. "Teachers and children from schools up and down the country have taken part in this study," the man was saying. What was he talking about?

Then suddenly, the man changed into a fox! The fox was walking on a roof. Next, Frisk saw some fox cubs playing in an empty house, and some other ones eating from a fox bin.

And then he saw something even more exciting. It was a fox cub with its head stuck in a can. A lot of children were crowding around the cub.

"Look, that's me!" said Jenny, and in the magic box Frisk saw her pulling the can off the fox cub's nose. Frisk's tail began to swish with excitement – he was looking at himself!

He saw himself again and again – looking through the window of the big building, trotting along the railway bank, and playing with the other cubs in the bramble patch. Then he saw Mom tipping over the fox milk and his brother and sister eating from the fox table.

We're on the magic box!

Frisk's tail swished harder than ever, and it knocked something off a little table.

Once more, three things happened
at once.

The cat
jumped down,

the people
turned around,

and the foxes
turned into children!

Frisk ran out
of the room. He
bounded through
the other room,
towards the fox flap.

But lying on the
floor in front of
the fox flap was
the dog.

Frisk didn't have time to think. There was
only one thing to do.

"The quick brown fox jumps over the lazy dog!" he said, and he jumped.

The dog woke up and barked, but it was too late. Frisk was already out through the fox flap. He was on his way home to tell Mom and the others that they were all magic foxes.